Puss in Boots

retold and illustrated by
Steve Light

Harry N. Abrams, Inc., Publishers

Long ago, a poor old miller died. He had little to leave to his three sons but his mill, his donkey, and his cat. The oldest son took the mill; the middle son took the donkey; and the youngest son got stuck, so he thought, with the cat.

"A cat!" said the youngest son, laughing and crying at the same time. "What in creation can I do with a cat but eat it and make a hat?"

"Not so fast!" said the cat. "Call the shoemaker and ask him to make me a pair of boots—a sturdy pair of boots so I can walk through the woods. Then you will know that you have won the greatest prize of all!"

Indeed, this cat had proven herself especially clever and cunning in the past. She was a great mouser, full of tricks to confuse the mice. So the young man persuaded the shoemaker to make a pair of boots for Puss, on credit.

Puss went stomping around the garden in her new boots. Then, when she was satisfied that they were a good fit, she went off to the woods, this time moving silently.

She carried a sack and some carrots, and using them she was able to capture a plump young rabbit.

Puss brought the kicking rabbit to the palace of the king. There she demanded an audience, and was ushered to the garden.

"Sire," she said, bowing low, "I bring you this rabbit, a gift from the Marquis of Carabas."

For that was the name she had invented for her penniless young master.
"Tell your master that I am glad to accept his gift," replied the king
graciously.

Soon the cat was making regular trips to the woods with her sack. Always she brought back some catch—a wild boar or a clutch of fine birds—and always she brought it directly to the king, as "a gift from the Marquis of Carabas."

The king was very pleased.

After a time, Puss and the king became quite friendly.

"I will not be home tomorrow," said the king one day. "I am taking my daughter, the princess, for a carriage ride along the river."

"Very good, Your Majesty," said the cat. Quickly she ran home.

"Master! Master!" she cried. "If you will swim in the river tomorrow, your fortune will be made!"

The next morning, Puss and her master went to the river, and the young man jumped in just where Puss suggested. Soon the king's carriage drew near, and Puss began to cry, "Help! Someone help! The Marquis of Carabas is drowning!"

The king regally put his head out the carriage window, and the lovely
princess put her head out regally, too. The king recognized the cat who had
so often brought him gifts, and he told his driver and footman to rescue the
Marquis of Carabas at once.

With her master safely on the riverbank, Puss explained to the king that while the Marquis was swimming, robbers had come and taken his clothes.

"Poor fellow," said the king sympathetically. And he sent his footman home to get a fine suit of clothes for the Marquis.

The king's clothes did wonders for the cat's poor master. The king invited the handsome young man to join them in the carriage. The princess looked at him with new interest, and their eyes met. Instantly they fell in love.

Puss had no time for love—she had work to do! She ran ahead until she saw
two peasants working in a field. She called to them, "Tell the king that all this
land belongs to the Marquis of Carabas, and you will be richly rewarded!"

There was no time to argue. The carriage approached. "Whose land is this,
my good men?" called the king.

"It belongs to the Marquis of Carabas," answered the men, for who knew
how rich the rewards of a talking cat could be? Her boots seemed very well made.

"You have inherited some nice property," said the king to the Marquis.

"It is surprisingly productive, sire," said the young Marquis.

Again and again this happened, with Puss in Boots running ahead to peasants in fields and by streams, planting seeds and herding cows, shoeing horses and feeding chickens. Always they told the king that their land, their seeds, their cows and horses and chickens were all owned by the great Marquis of Carabas.

The king was very impressed.

At last Puss, still running ahead, reached a castle owned by a terrible ogre. Not only was this ogre terrible—he was also very rich. In fact, he owned all the lands that the cat had claimed for the Marquis.

Puss knocked on the door.

"Come in, come in. Won't you sit down?" said the ogre. He looked at Puss hungrily.

Puss flicked her tail and took a seat. "This is a nice castle you have here, ogre," she observed.

"Thank you," said the ogre. "It's simple, but it's home."

"And I understand that you have some wonderful powers," said Puss. "I have heard that you can change yourself into any kind of animal— a lion or an elephant, even."

The ogre bowed his head modestly.

And then he turned into a lion!

"Rooooaaarrr!" the lion cried.

"Oh, dear!" Puss exclaimed, making her voice tremble. The ogre lion seemed pleased.

"Now I have also heard that you can transform yourself into the tiniest of animals—little mice or rats," continued Puss. "That seems completely impossible to me."

In answer, the ogre turned into a mouse. And instantly Puss in Boots
pounced and ate him up.

Just in time! Already she heard the rumbling of the king's carriage.
She ran downstairs, her boots thumping on the stairs.

Puss threw the gates of the castle wide.
  "Welcome, Your Majesty! Welcome to the castle of the Marquis of
Carabas!" she said.

That night there was a wonderful banquet at the king's palace, in honor of
the Marquis of Carabas. Everyone danced and sang and toasted the handsome
young Marquis—but he had eyes for no one but the beautiful princess.

At last the Marquis proposed a toast of his own. Turning to the princess, he
said, "Will you marry me, dear princess?"

"Yes, yes, I will, dear Marquis," murmured the princess. Everyone rejoiced, especially the king. He had quickly grown quite fond of the Marquis.

But perhaps Puss was the most pleased of all. For she had a kind and happy master, who was able to keep her in comfort—and in sturdy boots— for all her days.

To David J. Passalacqua, my teacher, mentor, and friend, who taught me how to learn.
I'd also like to thank Margaret Hurst, Veronica Lawlor, and Charlotte Noruzi
for their inspiration, encouragement, support, and advice.
Thanks, Mom and Jim, Dad and Cathy.
Thanks, Howard, for seeing the illustration in my art.

As an art teacher for three- to six-year-olds, I encourage my students to examine the art of respected artists as the children pursue their own artistic endeavors. As they look at the work of Paul Klee, Pablo Picasso, Andy Warhol, Henri Matisse, and Keith Haring, among others, or perhaps at a piece of folk art, I ask them to think about the process that went into the art. Then the children and I work together to create something new and fresh—yet something that draws upon the past. Recently I showed my five-year-olds a quilt and then taught them to sew using large needles and heavy thread. Together we made a quilt, with each child contributing a square.

In this same manner, I created the artwork for this book. I first studied the French Rococo artists, especially Jean-Honoré Fragonard, as well as French decorative wallpapers. I then made hand-stamped patterned paper in varying colors and shades, so I would have many to choose from as I worked on the pictures. I collaged the main illustrations on these patterned papers, using pencil to clarify outlines and to add detail as well as a feeling of spontaneity. Puss came to life when I found a piece of rich French provincial fabric, stained and worn with time, that evoked her poor past as well as her intellect and sophistication.

Like the children I teach, I took a celebrated art form as my inspiration, then added my favorite childhood story, *Puss in Boots*, to create my own world.

—Steve Light

Designer : Becky Terhune

Library of Congress Cataloging-in-Publication Data

Light, Steven.
Puss in boots / retold by Steve Light.
p. cm.
Summary : A clever cat helps her poor master win fame, fortune,
and the hand of a beautiful princess.
ISBN 0-8109-4368-9
[1. Fairy tales. 2. Folklore—France.] I. Puss in boots. English. II.
Title.
PZ8.L53 Pu 2002
398.2'0944'04529752—dc21
2001003746

Harry N. Abrams, Inc.
100 Fifth Avenue
New York, N.Y. 10011
www.abramsbooks.com

Abrams is a subsidiary of
LA MARTINIÈRE
GROUPE